The Adventure Continues . . .

Hi I'm Jackie. I'm an archeologist. I study ancient treasures to learn about the past.

My big adventure began when I found an eight-sided stone with a rooster on it. It was a magical charm—a talisman!

A legend says that there are twelve talismans scattered around the world—one for each animal in the Chinese zodiac. Each one holds a different kind of magic. All twelve together have incredible power!

An evil group called The Dark Hand wants to use the magic of talismans to rule the world. That's why I have to find them first.

I am really glad when my niece, Jade, discovers the monkey talisman. Until it gets stolen . . . by a monkey!

A PARACHUTE PRESS BOOK

TM and © 2002 Adelaide Productions, Inc. All Rights Reserved.

Published by Grosset & Dunlap, a division of Penguin Putnam Books for Young Readers, New York. GROSSET & DUNLAP is a trademark of Penguin Putnam, Inc. Published simultaneously in Canada. Printed in U.S.A.

Library of Congress Control Number: 2002106662

ISBN 0-448-42703-6
A B C D E F G H I J

JACKIE CHAN ADVENTURES ™ #11

The Jade Monkey

A novelization by Judy Katschke
based on the teleplay "The Jade Monkey"
written by David Slack

Grosset & Dunlap

Chapter 1

Eleven-year-old Jade sat behind her desk and grinned. It was Career Day in Ms. Hardman's class. And Jade's uncle, Jackie, was about to speak to the kids about ninjas, magic talismans, and fighting an evil group called The Dark Hand!

"Hey, Jade," her classmate, Drew, whispered. "Is your uncle going to talk about being a secret agent today?" He started to laugh.

"You bet he is!" Jade said. "And the truth is going to blow your mind!" She knew Drew didn't believe Jackie was a secret agent. But he would after today!

Jackie stepped to the front of the classroom. "Hi, kids," he said. "I'm Jackie Chan. I'm an archaeologist. I search for ancient artifacts. Artifacts are objects left by people who lived long ago. But my job isn't easy. I have to dig through dirt with tiny brushes. . . ."

The kids yawned and shuffled in their seats.

What is Jackie doing up there? Jade wondered. He's not supposed to talk about boring archaeology. He's supposed to talk about his other job—working for a secret U.S. government agency called Section Thirteen. And helping them fight The Dark Hand!

"So much for the 'Secret Agent Man.'" Drew snickered.

That did it! Jade threw her hand up in the air. "Jackie!" she called. "Tell us about the time you whomped a bunch of Shadowkhan warriors on a roller coaster!"

Jackie's eyes opened wide. "Um," he said. "That's a bit off the topic, Jade. Now, once I find an artifact, I take my brush and—"

Jade stood up and faced her classmates. "But Jackie is also a secret agent!" she cried. "He's got amazing reflexes. Watch this!" She yanked an apple from her lunch bag and hurled it at Jackie.

But instead of seeing him karate-chop it into a million pieces—

Bonk! The apple bounced off Jackie's head.

"Ow!" he yelled.

Ms. Hardman frowned. "Jade has quite an imagination, doesn't she, Mr. Chan?" she asked.

"Yes, she does," Jackie said, rubbing his head. "And she has a good throwing arm, too."

Jade slumped into her seat. Now no one will believe me, she thought. She folded her arms across her chest while Jackie finished his speech.

"And that's what it's like to be an archaeologist," Jackie said to the class.

4

He walked to the back of the room and sat next to Jade.

"Thanks a lot, Jackie," Jade said. "You made me look like a big fat liar. Why didn't you talk about Section Thirteen?"

"I couldn't do that, Jade. My work with Section Thirteen is a big secret, remember?" Jackie whispered. "Besides, this is Career Day, right? And my career is archaeology."

"Well, next time we go on a mission, I'm bringing back proof of what you really do!" Jade said.

"*Next* time?" Jackie replied. "There won't *be* a next time. You're not supposed to go on assignments with me, Jade."

"But—" Jade began.

Jackie cut her off. "*Shhh*. The teacher is talking."

"Class, next week I'd like *you* to report on a family member's job," Ms. Hardman said. "After you go to work with him or her."

Jackie groaned. "I don't believe this."

A huge smile spread across Jade's face. Yes! she thought. Now Jackie *has* to let me go on a mission with him. I can get all the proof I need!

Chapter 2

"Awesome!" Jade said from inside her scuba mask. She and Jackie were underwater, searching for another magic talisman.

Jackie and Jade dived deeper and deeper into the ocean. They wore full scuba gear fitted with built-in microphones. Zillions of colorful fish were swimming right past their faces!

"Still think archaeology is boring?" Jackie asked.

"No way!" Jade said. They were looking at the sunken ruins of an ancient temple. Jade pulled out her underwater camera and snapped a picture.

"We'll start looking here," Jackie said. "But remember, Jade. Finding the talisman could take hours."

"Right," Jade said. She noticed a lump on the ocean floor. She brushed aside some sand. Underneath the cloud of silt was an eight-sided stone. It was a talisman!

"Oh, Jackie?" Jade called with a smile. She held up the talisman.

"You've got to be kidding me!" Jackie cried. "I can't believe you found it so quickly."

Jade took a closer look at the talisman. There was a black monkey carved in the center of the stone. "It's the monkey talisman!" she said happily. "Must be a *sea* monkey."

Just then Jade spotted three scuba divers swimming toward them.

Jackie saw the divers at the same time. "It's Finn, Ratso, and Chow!" he exclaimed.

Jade's stomach did a triple-flip. Finn, Ratso, and Chow were members of The Dark Hand—a dangerous group of thugs. Its evil enforcers would stop at nothing to get a talisman!

With the monkey talisman in her hand, Jade swam away as fast as she could. But she wasn't fast enough. Ratso grabbed her.

9

"Jackieeeee!" Jade shouted.

Jackie lunged at Ratso with a flying kick.

"Ugh!" Ratso grunted. The kick sent him reeling through the deep water. He lost his grip on Jade's arm, and she was free.

"Jade, get back into the boat," Jackie ordered.

"Okay," Jade said. She clutched the talisman and began to swim to the surface.

Meanwhile, the battle between Jackie and The Dark Hand enforcers raged on.

Jackie dodged through the under-water ruins. Finn, Ratso, and Chow were close behind him.

Suddenly, Chow pulled out a

sword—and sliced through Jackie's air hose!

Oh no, Jackie thought in horror. He bolted to the surface and yanked off his mask. But just as he took a breath, Ratso dragged him back underwater.

Jackie had to think fast. He slipped off his scuba tank and hit Ratso with a single swing.

While Jackie and the enforcer struggled underwater, Jade crawled into the boat. She smiled at the monkey talisman still in her hand.

Then she saw a huge, dark shadow loom over the deck. Jade looked up and gasped. "Tohru!"

Tohru was The Dark Hand's mightiest enforcer.

"The talisman," Tohru ordered, holding out his hand.

Then Jade saw Finn, Ratso, and Chow climb aboard the boat. Her heart began to pound. Where are you, Jackie? she wondered. I need your help!

She slowly backed away from the three enforcers. "You guys are going down!" she cried, trying to sound tough.

"You can't beat us." Ratso snickered. "You're just a little girl!"

Splash! A huge wave broke over the deck. The boat rocked wildly. It knocked the thugs off their feet, but Jade kept her balance.

"Told you!" Jade said. She ran to the other end of the boat.

The enforcers stumbled in their

12

flippers as they chased her across the deck.

Just then Jackie jumped into the boat. "Stop!" he cried.

Finn, Ratso, Chow, and Tohru froze for a second.

"Hey, we don't have to listen to you," Finn said. The four men turned to fight Jackie.

Kicking, chopping, and blocking, Jackie put up a good fight.

But then Tohru grabbed him. He lifted Jackie high above his head.

"Jackieeee!" Jade shouted. She had to do something. But what? She looked down at the talisman in her hand.

I know! she thought. I'll use the magic of the talisman to help.

13

But Jade had no idea what the monkey talisman did. What if its power was dangerous?

"Oh, well." Jade closed her eyes and squeezed the talisman. "Monkey magic better be good. . . ."

Chapter 3

Jade opened her eyes. "Hey, nothing happened!" she cried. "How does this thing work, anyway?"

Jade tried everything to power up the monkey talisman.

She shook it. She rubbed it. She even blew on it. Still, nothing.

The waves rocked the boat back and forth. Jade started to feel a little queasy. "Come on!" she told the talisman. "Activate already before this boat ride makes me *yack!*"

A beam of light shot out from the talisman. It hit Jackie and—

Zap! It turned him into a woolly, long-horned *yak!*

"Whoa!" Jade gasped. "That's not what I had in mind."

"What just happened here?" Finn demanded.

"Chan's a yak," Chow answered.

"He sure is," Ratso said.

Tohru pointed a beefy finger at Jade. "The talisman!" he grunted.

Jackie-the-yak charged toward the enforcers. With his sturdy horns, he rammed into the goons from behind.

"Aughh!" they yelled as they flew overboard.

Jade cheered. Jackie's new horns

came in handy. But he couldn't stay a yak forever.

"Change him back!" she ordered the talisman.

Another beam shot out from the charm. Jade smiled as Jackie zapped back into a human.

"Totally cool!" Jade exclaimed. "This must be the turn-stuff-into-other-stuff talisman!"

"I noticed." Jackie sighed, rubbing his head.

Jade felt the boat rock again. But this time it wasn't the ocean making waves. It was Tohru!

The giant pulled himself back onto the boat. He snarled as he lumbered aboard and lunged toward Jackie and Jade.

"Jade!" Jackie said, tugging her sleeve. "Use the talisman!"

With a shaky hand, she aimed the monkey talisman at Tohru. "How about if I turn Tohru into a . . . "

The deck began to tilt. Jackie and Jade looked up and gulped. Even Tohru gasped.

A fifty-foot wave was crashing toward the boat!

"Waaaaaa!" the three yelled.

Crash!

The massive wave hit the boat and knocked it upside down!

Chapter 4

Jade lay flat on her back. Her head was spinning. "Where am I?" she moaned.

Jade opened her eyes. She saw fluffy white clouds, a bright blue sky, a monkey. . . .

"A *monkey?*" Jade gasped.

"Eep! Eep! Eep!" A spiky-haired monkey leaned over Jade's face and chattered. His breath was stinky.

"Hel-lo? How about using some

mouthwash?" Jade gently pushed the monkey away and sat up.

She was still wearing her rubber scuba suit. Her camera was around her neck and the monkey talisman was in her hand.

She looked around and saw palm trees, tropical flowers, and a white sandy beach. That could only mean one thing.

"I'm shipwrecked!" Jade cheered happily. "My school report is going to rock!"

"Eep! Eep!" The monkey jumped up and down.

"I think I'll call you Gus," Jade said. She pointed her camera at the monkey. "Now, say cheese!"

Gus's long, fuzzy arm snatched at

the monkey talisman in her hand.

"Hey, that's not for you," Jade said, holding it away from him. "Even if it *does* have your picture on it."

Jade sat silently for a moment. Where was Jackie? She had to find him. With Gus at her heels, she left the beach and began to search the jungle.

"Jackie!" Jade called. "Jackie!"

No answer.

Then Jade heard a loud splash. She spun around to see the four Dark Hand enforcers. They were stumbling out of the lagoon onto the beach.

"Oh, no!" Jade groaned.

"Eep! Eep! Eep!" Gus screeched, jumping up and down.

Tohru looked up and spotted Jade.

"The girl! She's in the jungle," he told the others. "Get her!"

"Got to go!" Jade said, running away from Finn, Ratso, Chow, and Tohru.

"Eep! Eep! Eep!" The little monkey climbed onto a tree limb. He followed Jade by swinging from tree to tree.

"What am I going to do?" Jade moaned. She felt the talisman tucked in her palm. "Duh! Use the turn-things-into-other-things talisman!"

Jade skidded to a stop behind a fallen hollow log. Maybe I can turn this into a weapon, she thought. She picked it up.

"Turn this log into a super-duper stinging laser ray!" she commanded the talisman. She pointed the charm at the log.

Zap! Jade wasn't holding a laser ray—she was holding a flapping, flopping *manta* ray!

"Change it back!" Jade yelled. "Change it back!"

Zap! The wiggling sea creature turned back into a log.

"Guess it only does animals," she told Gus. "In that case . . ."

Jade aimed the monkey talisman at The Dark Hand enforcers closing in on her.

"Okay," Jade said. "How about if I get these *rats* off my tail?"

The beam shot out and blasted Ratso. In a flash he was turned into an ugly rat.

"Ratso!" Finn exclaimed. He picked up the rat and stuffed it into his pocket. "We'll get you for this!" he cried, continuing the chase.

But Jade would not give up. She aimed the talisman again. "Aardvark!" she shouted over her shoulder as she began to run. "Hippo! Giraffe!"

The thugs ducked and dodged. The beams struck a boulder, a bush, and one of Gus's monkey friends.

Soon Jade was staring at an aardvark statue, a bush shaped like a hippo, and a giraffe.

Oops! Well, at least the giraffe is real! Jade thought. She ducked behind a tree and looked around. "I've got to find a place to hide."

Gus yanked a juicy fruit from the tree. He began to chomp loudly.

Now what? Jade wondered. She

looked at Gus, then looked at the talisman. Then she got the most major idea ever!

"Double-duh!" Jade said. She pointed the talisman at her chest. "Make a *monkey* out of me!"

Zap! Jade felt an enormous jolt. Then she felt . . . sort of hairy.

"It worked! It worked!" Jade cried. She wiggled her tail behind her. "I'm a monkey!"

Monkey Jade leaped into the tree next to Gus. She gave him a little monkey-wave.

"Eep! Eep!" Jade chattered. "Eep! Eep! Eep!"

She watched Chow, Finn, and Tohru race past the tree.

"Where did she go?" Tohru asked.

"This way, I think!" Finn said.

They ran deeper into the jungle.

"That was close," Jade said. "But this fur is starting to itch." She pointed the talisman toward her chest again. "So change me—"

"Eep!" Gus screeched. He snatched the talisman from Jade and began to sniff it.

"Eep! Eep! Eep!" Jade scolded him. She grabbed for the talisman, but Gus was too quick. He leaped out of sight as Jade tumbled to the ground.

"Oof!" Jade grunted. She turned and saw Gus scamper away with the talisman. How was she supposed to change back to a girl without it?

Not good, Jade thought glumly. *Way* not good!

Chapter 5

I've got to get that talisman back,
Jade thought. Or else I'll be a monkey
forever! She used her long, monkey
arms to help her scamper to the top
of a tree.

Jade could see for miles from the
treetop. But what she *heard* made her
ears perk up.

"Jade!" a voice called. "Where are
you?"

That's Jackie! Jade thought. He's

looking for me! If I follow his voice, I bet I'll find him! She scampered down the tree. Together, we'll be able to find the monkey talisman—and turn me back into *me* again!

I have to find Jade, Jackie thought as he wandered through the jungle. He stopped when he spotted something shiny on the ground.

It was Jade's underwater camera. And next to it were two enormous footprints!

"Jade was here!" Jackie cried, picking up the camera. He looked at the footprints and frowned. "And so was Tohru."

Jackie carefully followed the trail of footprints.

"Eep! Eep! Eep!"

A screeching monkey dropped to the ground right in front of him.

"Whoa there, little monkey," Jackie said.

But it wasn't just any monkey. It was Jade!

"Jackie!" Jade cried. "I'm so glad I found you. Those Dark Hand guys were after me, so I turned into a monkey, and then this other monkey took the talisman, and—"

"Shoo!" Jackie said. He waved a hand. "Go away, monkey."

Jade stared at Jackie. What was his problem? Didn't he hear what she just said?

Then she got it. Monkeys don't speak English, Jade realized. Jackie

29

doesn't understand a single word I'm saying!

But Jade wasn't going to give up. If Jackie couldn't understand monkey-talk, maybe he would understand charades!

Okay, Jade thought. First word. Sounds like *maid.*

Jade picked up a feathery plant. She began dusting the ground with it. *Maid . . . Jade.* Get it?

Jackie stared at the monkey blankly. "You seem like a very nice monkey," he said. "But I have to find Jade."

"Wait!" Jade jumped on top of Jackie's head. She began to screech. "Don't go!"

"Hey! Cut it out! Stop it right

now, monkey!" Jackie yelled.

Jade didn't know what to do next. How was she ever going to convince Jackie that she was a monkey?

Then Jade spotted her camera in Jackie's hands. That's it!

She leaped down and grabbed her camera. She pointed at the camera, then at herself.

"Forget it, monkey," Jackie said. "I'm not going to take your picture. I have to go."

"No!" Jade cried. She pointed to her name on the camera. "See? It says Jade right there!"

Jackie's eyes popped wide open. "You know where Jade is?" he asked. "What happened to her?"

Excited, Jade grabbed a twig. She

drew an arrow in the dirt. She was about to jump in front of the arrow when Jackie cried out.

"An arrow!" he exclaimed. He patted Jade on her fuzzy head. "Thank you, little monkey!"

Jade watched in horror as Jackie followed the arrow into the jungle. "No!" Jade cried. "Not that way, Jackie. I'm right over here!" She started after him.

"Eep! Eep!" A pair of large monkey hands snatched up Jade. And they didn't belong to Gus. They belonged to a bigger monkey!

"Hey!" Jade cried. "Put me down! Put me down!"

The monkey carried Jade deeper and deeper into the jungle. When

32

they reached a busy monkey habitat, the big monkey dropped Jade to the ground.

Jade looked at all the baby monkeys around her and groaned. Oh, great, she thought. This monkey thinks she's my mother!

Mama Monkey held Jade in place with her big feet. She smiled as she picked and plucked through the fur on Jade's arm.

"Whoa!" Jade shouted. "What are you doing?"

Mama Monkey yanked a bug from Jade's fur. Then she popped it right into her mouth!

"Gross!" Jade cried. Using all her strength, Jade broke away and scurried into the jungle.

Mama Monkey let out an ear-splitting, *"Eeeeeeep!"*

"Guess that means 'see you later' in monkey," Jade said. Then she froze. An entire family of angry monkeys blocked her path!

"Um . . . guess not."

Chapter 6

Meanwhile, Jackie was lost. "This is the last time I follow directions from a monkey," he said as he wandered through the forest.

Jackie stopped when he heard voices. He peeked through the brush and spotted Chow, Finn, and Tohru. The Dark Hand enforcers were surrounding a monkey perched on a boulder.

"Don't move!" Chow told Gus. "Stay there!"

"Eep! Eep!" Gus cried.

Jackie's jaw dropped. The monkey was holding the monkey talisman!

"Nobody is going to hurt you," Finn said.

But before the thugs could grab the monkey, Jackie leaped forward. "Hee-yaaaa!"

"Eep!" Gus screeched. He jumped off the rock and scurried away.

"The monkey!" Tohru shouted. "Catch it, quick!"

The enforcers began to chase the monkey.

Jackie reached out and yanked Finn back. "Tell me where Jade is," he demanded.

Finn gave Jackie a push.

Jackie responded with a fierce kick.

36

Something gray and furry popped out of Finn's pocket.

"Ratso!" Finn cried. In a panic, he ran after the squeaking rat.

Jackie's eyes widened. "That's . . . *Ratso?*"

Finn tried to catch the runaway rat.

But Jackie was faster. He snatched Ratso and held him up by his long, skinny tail.

"Tell me what you've done with Jade, Finn," Jackie demanded. "Or Ratso here gets it."

Ratso-the-rat squirmed. "Squeak! Squeak! Squeak!"

"Calm down, dude!" Finn told Jackie. "We were chasing her. The kid zapped Ratso. And the next thing we knew that monkey had the talisman!"

Jackie stared at the rat, trying to figure out what had happened.

"Jade turned Ratso into a rat . . . and turned *herself* into a monkey!" he said slowly.

Jackie tossed the rat to Finn. Then he joined the chase for the runaway monkey.

"Jade!" Jackie called.

They ran through the jungle.

Bonk! A mango hit Chow on the head.

Jackie looked up and saw a fruit-tossing monkey high in a tree. "Eep! Eep! Eep!"

The enforcers yelled and ducked as the monkey pelted them with mangoes, papayas, and bananas.

Jade always did have a good

throwing arm, Jackie thought. Maybe that's her! He scaled the towering tree and settled on a branch.

"Here, Jade!" Jackie said, reaching out his arm. "It's me. Jackie!"

The monkey looked up from the fruit it was chewing. Then it let out a huge burp.

Jackie frowned. Jade had more manners than that!

The monkey grabbed a vine and swung to another tree.

"Jade!" Jackie yelled as he followed. "Quit fooling around!" Finally, he caught up to the monkey. He reached out and grabbed the talisman. "Sorry, Jade!" he said. "This is for your own good."

Jackie aimed the talisman at the

monkey. "Change her back!" he ordered. He waited for the talisman to zap the monkey back into his niece.

But nothing happened!

Chapter 7

Jackie aimed the monkey talisman again. "Change her back!" he cried. But still, it didn't work.

"Did you break the talisman, Jade?" Jackie asked the monkey.

"Gotcha!" Finn snatched the monkey talisman from Jackie's hand.

Jackie whirled around. The Dark Hand enforcers had followed him up the tree!

Before he could do anything,

Tohru grabbed him in a bear hug.

Jackie grunted and strained but could not break the giant's grip.

"Here goes nothing!" Finn said. He pointed the talisman at the rat on his shoulder.

Zap! The rat turned back into Ratso.

Ratso's weight pulled his friend to the ground. "Oof!" Finn grunted as Ratso dropped on top of him.

Jackie didn't get it. The talisman wasn't broken. So why didn't it work on Jade?

At that moment Tohru surprised Jackie with a paralyzing nerve pinch!

Jackie's knees weakened as he began to black out. . . .

On the other side of the jungle, Jade had her own problems. She was up to her neck in swamp water—and monkey business.

"Stop it!" Jade shouted. "I don't need a bath!"

Mama Monkey smiled as she dunked Jade into the stream.

Jade wriggled out of her hands and began to swim away.

"Eep! Eep! Eep!" Mama Monkey screeched. She clawed under the water for her baby.

But Jade was already halfway down the stream.

Jade's monkey-fur dripped as she climbed out of the water. "Later, Mom," Jade whispered as she sneaked away.

She had to find Jackie and the talisman. Before things *really* got hairy!

Jackie moaned as he came to. Shaking off his daze, he found himself tied to a large rock. A monkey was tied to the rock, too.

"Jade?" Jackie whispered.

Ratso, Finn, Chow, and Tohru were talking just a few feet away.

"I say we turn him into a dog!" Ratso said. "I like dogs!"

Finn bounced the talisman in his palm. "Why would you want to turn him into something you like?" he demanded.

"How about a cockroach?" Chow snickered. "So we can *stomp* him!"

Oh, no, Jackie thought. They're

planning to use the talisman on *me!*

Tohru grabbed the talisman from Finn. "Perhaps an animal we can eat?" he suggested.

"Mmm!" Chow laughed. "Chicken à la Chan!"

"Noooo!" Jackie shouted as he struggled against the rope.

Tohru aimed the talisman at Jackie. "Say good-bye, Chan."

Just then, another monkey swung out on a vine. "Eeeeeeeeeeeeeep!" It grabbed the talisman from Tohru with its hairy feet.

Jackie gasped as the monkey landed in front of him.

"Eep, eep, eep!" the monkey said. *Zap!*

Right before Jackie's eyes, the

45

monkey was changed into a human girl . . . Jade!

"Hi!" Jade said with a little wave.

"Jade?" Jackie was stunned. He turned to the monkey next to him. "Then who are *you*?"

"Burrrp," Gus replied.

"No time for introductions," Jade said. She untied Jackie just in time to fight off The Dark Hand.

Ratso, Chow, and Finn swung their fists. Jackie twirled, kicked, and blocked their explosive punches.

Meanwhile, Tohru marched toward Jade. "Give me the talisman!" he demanded.

"No way!" Jade cried. She aimed the talisman at Tohru and cried, "Elephant!"

Zap!

Jade smiled at her quick think-ing—until the huge elephant began charging Jackie!

"Jade!" Jackie cried as he ran. "Bad move! Bad move!"

"Oops," Jade said. She saw Ratso rushing toward her. Then she got an idea. "Elephants are afraid of *rats!*"

She aimed the talisman at Ratso and zapped him back into a big fat rat!

Tohru-the-elephant skidded to a stop when he saw the rat. He hopped onto a boulder and shivered with fear.

Jade laughed out loud. And Chow plucked the talisman right out of her hand!

"Jackie!" Jade yelled.

Chow zapped Ratso and Tohru back into their regular bodies. Then he turned to Jackie and shouted, "You're a *flamingo!*"

Jackie ducked. The beam missed Jackie and zapped Tohru into a bright pink flamingo!

Jade yanked the talisman from Chow's hand. She turned and saw Finn and Ratso charging at her.

There wasn't enough time to zap all three goons. So Jade decided to zap Jackie instead.

She pointed the talisman at her uncle and shouted, "Kangaroo!"

"Huh?" Jackie cried.

Zap! Jackie became a kangaroo. A *boxing* kangaroo!

Jackie stopped all three of the

thugs with one mighty punch.

"Good choice!" Jade said happily. She didn't realize that a pink flamingo was sneaking up behind her.

"Hey!" Jade cried as the flamingo's beak snatched the talisman away from her.

Horrified, Jade watched as the flamingo turned back into Tohru. The giant smiled an evil smile, then pointed the talisman at Jade.

"Rabbit!" he commanded.

"Noooo!" Jade groaned. In a flash she had bunny ears and a fluffy cottontail.

Tohru snickered. He didn't see the kangaroo sneak up behind *him!*

Whack! Jackie kicked the talisman out of Tohru's hands—and caught it

49

in his kangaroo pouch!

Jackie hopped away from the charging enforcers.

Jade bunny-hopped after him. But she wasn't fast enough. Jackie scooped her up and stuffed her into his pouch. Gus jumped onto Jackie's back and rode along.

Jackie hopped swiftly through the forest. He paused when he came upon a thick cluster of trees. Which way should they go?

"Eep! Eep! Eep!" Gus pointed behind them. The Dark Hand thugs were getting closer.

"Let's go!" Kangaroo-Jackie hopped through the brush as fast as he could. But then he stopped short and froze. "Whoa!"

They were standing on the edge of a steep cliff!

The Dark Hand enforcers filed onto the cliff, behind them. Jackie gulped. There was no where to go— but *down!*

Chapter 8

Snug in Jackie's kangaroo pouch, Jade stared down the steep drop of the cliff. Then she leaned out and looked back at the enforcers closing in on them. We have to use the talisman! she thought.

She ducked into Jackie's kangaroo pouch—and popped up with the talisman between her teeth.

Zap! Jackie and Jade were flashed back to normal.

But Jade wasn't finished yet.

"I hope this means what I think it means!" Jade told Gus. She cupped her hands around her mouth. Then she called the Mama Monkey's cry for help. "Eeeeeeeep! Eeeeeeeep!"

"Huh?" Chow cried.

The Dark Hand enforcers whirled around and yelped. Jade's whole monkey family was spilling out of the jungle!

"Eeeeeeeep! Eeeeeeeep! Eeeeeeeep!" the monkeys cried.

"Yes!" Jade cheered. "It worked!"

The thugs screamed as dozens of hairy little fists pummeled them.

"Hey! Ow! Cut it out!"

Jade and Gus cheered. The monkey brigade chased the enforcers into the forest and out of sight.

But one monkey wasn't going anywhere. Mama Monkey shook an angry finger at Gus. Then she turned to Jade and cooed.

"Hi, Mom," Jade said, smiling.

"Mom?" Jackie asked, surprised.

Mama Monkey leaped onto Jackie's shoulder.

Jackie's eyes bugged out as Mama Monkey searched his hair for bugs!

Jade grabbed her camera from around Jackie's neck and snapped a picture.

"I guess you're family, too, Jackie," she said, laughing.

Jade had a lot to be happy about. She had helped her uncle rescue the talisman from evil enemy villains.

54

She had even learned how to speak
"monkey."

But most of all, her school report
was going to *rock!*

A letter to you from Jackie

Dear Friends,

In _The Jade Monkey_, Jade gets a cool surprise when a family of monkeys saves us from The Dark Hand. How does it happen? It's simple. Jade takes a chance and asks for help.

Sometimes it's hard for us to take chances. We're afraid we might fail and so instead of risking failure, we just don't try.

I remember one time when I felt this way, too. It was many years ago, before I started making movies in the United States. My career wasn't going so well. I was passed from director to director in the hopes that one of them could figure out how to make me a star.

Deep down, I knew I didn't need the directors to tell me how to be a star. I had lots of good ideas. But I was too afraid to speak out.

Instead of talking to the directors with confidence, I timidly asked them to try some scenes my way. Not one director listened to me. Finally, I stopped giving my suggestions, thinking it would get me nowhere anyway.

Then I went to work with another new director. I

was very nervous. I knew that if we did the same old type of movie, it would be just as unsuccessful as the others. I had to get this director to listen to me.

So I took the chance. I worked up the courage and went to speak to him. I told him my ideas with confidence and assurance. And do you know what? He listened!

Not only that, he helped me develop my ideas into a concept called Kung Fu Comedy—the type of action movie that made me the star I am today!

So the next time you're afraid to take a chance—don't be! You never know what will happen!

Find out what happens in the next book!

SUPER SPECIAL
Day of the Dragon

A dangerous group called The Dark Hand steals twelve magical talismans. Now they have the power to unleash a horrible force of evil—and rule the world! it's up to Jackie to stop them—but how?